Let's Look at Sunflowers

Katie Peters

GRL Consultants,
Diane Craig and Monica Marx,
Certified Literacy Specialists

Pull Ahead Readers

Lerner Publications ◆ Minneapolis

Note from a GRL Consultant
This Pull Ahead leveled book has been carefully designed for beginning readers. A team of guided reading literacy experts has reviewed and leveled the book to ensure readers pull ahead and experience success.

Lerner Publications Company
An imprint of Lerner Publishing Group, Inc.
241 First Avenue North
Minneapolis, MN 55401 USA

For reading levels and more information, look up this title at www.lernerbooks.com.

Main body text set in Memphis Pro 24/39
Typeface provided by Linotype.

Photo Acknowledgments
The images in this book are used with the permission of: © AlexeyVS/iStockphoto, pp. 10, 11, 16 (bud); © bonchan/iStockphoto, p. 3; © ClarkandCompany/iStockphoto, pp. 4, 5, 16 (seeds); © Harry Wedzinga/iStockphoto, pp. 8, 9; © JosephJacobs/iStockphoto, pp. 6, 7; © Pee Tongsadayu/iStockphoto, pp. 14, 15, 16 (bee); © tomch/iStockphoto, pp. 12, 13, 16 (sunflower).

Front cover: © ohishiistk/iStockphoto

Library of Congress Cataloging-in-Publication Data

Names: Peters, Katie, author.
Title: Let's look at sunflowers / Katie Peters.
Description: Minneapolis : Lerner Publications, [2021] | Series: Plant life cycles (pull ahead readers - nonfiction) | Includes index. | Audience: Ages 4–7 | Audience: Grades K–1 | Summary: "Sunflowers are a cheerful addition to any bouquet. What does it look like while it is growing? This title shows younger readers how with full-color photos. Pairs with the fiction title Flowers in the Sun."— Provided by publisher.
Identifiers: LCCN 2019046373 (print) | LCCN 2019046374 (ebook) | ISBN 9781541590229 (library binding) | ISBN 9781728403168 (paperback) | ISBN 9781728400785 (ebook)
Subjects: LCSH: Sunflowers—Life cycles—Juvenile literature.
Classification: LCC QK495.C74 P485 2021 (print) | LCC QK495.C74 (ebook) | DDC 583/.983—dc23

LC record available at https://lccn.loc.gov/2019046373
LC ebook record available at https://lccn.loc.gov/2019046374

Manufactured in the United States of America
4-1011198-48076-10/13/2025

Contents

Let's Look at Sunflowers

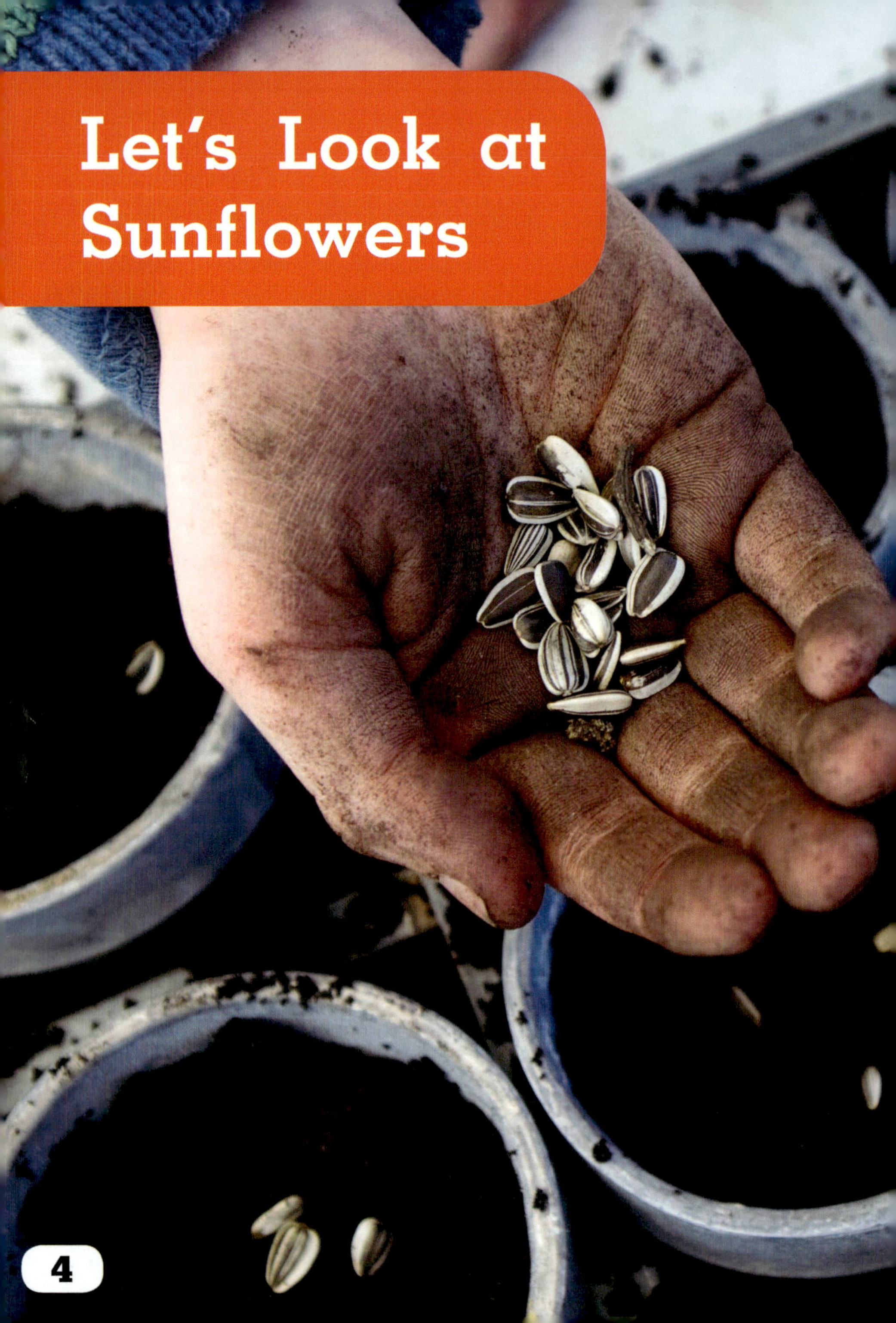

Here are sunflower seeds.

A sunflower plant grows out of each seed.

A sunflower plant grows a tall stem.

A sunflower bud grows on the stem.

A sunflower bud grows into a sunflower.

Bees like the sunflower. New seeds grow in the sunflower.

Did You See It?

bee

sunflower

sunflower bud

sunflower seeds

Index